THIS BOOK

BELONGS TO:

THE TALE OF
Tom Kitten

FREDERICK WARNE

Published by the Penguin Group
Penguin Books Ltd, 80 Strand, London WC2R ORL, England
Penguin Putnam Inc., 375 Hudson Street, New York, New York 10014, USA
Penguin Books Australia Ltd, 250 Camberwell Road, Camberwell, Victoria 3124, Australia
Penguin Books Canada Ltd, 10 Alcorn Avenue, Toronto, Ontario, Canada M4V 3B2
Penguin Books India (P) Ltd, 11 Community Centre,
Panchsheel Park, New Delhi 110 017, India
Penguin Books (NZ) Ltd, Cnr Rosedale and Airborne Roads,
Albany, Auckland, New Zealand
Penguin Books (South Africa) (Pty) Ltd, PO Box 9, Parklands 2121, South Africa

Penguin Books Ltd, Registered Offices: 80 Strand, London WC2R ORL, England

Web site at: www.peterrabbit.com

First published by Frederick Warne 1907
This edition with reset text and new reproductions of Beatrix Potter's
illustrations first published 2002

Colour reproduction by
EAE Creative Colour Ltd, Norwich
Printed and bound in Italy

THE TALE OF
TOM KITTEN

BY

BEATRIX POTTER

Alameda Free Library
1550 Oak Street
Alameda, CA 94501

FREDERICK WARNE

DEDICATED TO ALL

PICKLES

— ESPECIALLY TO THOSE THAT GET

UPON MY GARDEN WALL

O̲NCE UPON A TIME there were three little kittens, and their names were —

Mittens,
Tom Kitten,
and Moppet.

They had dear little fur coats of their own; and they tumbled about the doorstep and played in the dust.

BUT one day their mother — Mrs. Tabitha Twitchit — expected friends to tea; so she fetched the kittens indoors, to wash and dress them, before the fine company arrived.

FIRST she scrubbed their faces (this one is Moppet).

THEN she brushed their fur
(this one is Mittens).

14

THEN she combed their tails and whiskers (this is Tom Kitten).

Tom was very naughty, and he scratched.

MRS. TABITHA dressed Moppet and Mittens in clean pinafores and tuckers; and then she took all sorts of elegant uncomfortable clothes out of a chest of drawers, in order to dress up her son Thomas.

TOM KITTEN was very fat, and he had grown; several buttons burst off. His mother sewed them on again.

When the three kittens were ready, Mrs. Tabitha unwisely turned them out into the garden, to be out of the way while she made hot buttered toast.

"Now keep your frocks clean, children! You must walk on your hind legs. Keep away from the dirty ash-pit, and from Sally Henny-penny, and from the pig-stye and the Puddle-ducks."

MOPPET and Mittens walked down the garden path unsteadily. Presently they trod upon their pinafores and fell on their noses.

When they stood up there were several green smears!

"LET us climb up the rockery, and sit on the garden wall," said Moppet.

They turned their pinafores back to front, and went up with a skip and a jump; Moppet's white tucker fell down into the road.

TOM KITTEN was quite unable to jump when walking upon his hind legs in trousers. He came up the rockery by degrees, breaking the ferns, and shedding buttons right and left.

H E was all in pieces when he reached the top of the wall.

Moppet and Mittens tried to pull him together; his hat fell off, and the rest of his buttons burst.

WHILE they were in difficulties, there was a pit pat paddle pat! and the three Puddle-ducks came along the hard high road, marching one behind the other and doing the goose step — pit pat paddle pat! pit pat waddle pat!

THEY stopped and stood in a row, and stared up at the kittens. They had very small eyes and looked surprised.

THEN the two duck-birds, Rebeccah and Jemima Puddle-duck, picked up the hat and tucker and put them on.

MITTENS laughed so that she fell off the wall. Moppet and Tom descended after her; the pinafores and all the rest of Tom's clothes came off on the way down.

"Come! Mr. Drake Puddle-duck," said Moppet — "Come and help us to dress him! Come and button up Tom!"

MR. DRAKE PUDDLE-DUCK
advanced in a slow sideways
manner, and picked up the
various articles.

BUT he put them on *himself!* They fitted him even worse than Tom Kitten.

"It's a very fine morning!" said Mr. Drake Puddle-duck.

AND he and Jemima and Rebeccah
Puddle-duck set off up the road,
keeping step — pit pat, paddle pat!
pit pat, waddle pat!

THEN Tabitha Twitchit came down the garden and found her kittens on the wall with no clothes on.

SHE pulled them off the wall, smacked them, and took them back to the house.

"My friends will arrive in a minute, and you are not fit to be seen; I am affronted," said Mrs. Tabitha Twitchit.

SHE sent them upstairs; and I am sorry to say she told her friends that they were in bed with the measles; which was not true.

QUITE the contrary; they were not in bed; *not* in the least.

Somehow there were very extraordinary noises over-head, which disturbed the dignity and repose of the tea-party.

AND I think that some day I shall have to make another, larger, book, to tell you more about Tom Kitten!

53

As for the Puddle-ducks — they went into a pond.

The clothes all came off directly, because there were no buttons.

AND Mr. Drake Puddle-duck, and Jemima and Rebeccah, have been looking for them ever since.

THE END